DIWALI

Tulika Singh is a children's author and mother of two, dedicated to bringing stories of wisdom, heritage and culture to young minds. A graduate of Miranda House and an MBA by training, she brings with her a rich background from successful corporate stints abroad.

Currently, she devotes herself full-time to creating meaningful content for children through her platform, www.ashwathatreebooks.com, where she writes, curates and publishes stories rooted in Indian traditions and timeless values.

Through her storytelling, Tulika hopes to nurture curiosity, cultural pride and inner strength in every child.

To my Guru, Om Swami, who shows us that the brightest Diwali is the light of the soul within.

RED PANDA

DIWALI

STORIES, LEGENDS, MYTHS

TULIKA SINGH

ILLUSTRATED BY NIRZARA VERULKAR

RED
PANDA

Published by Red Panda, an imprint of Westland Books, a division of Nasadiya Technologies Private Limited, in 2025

No. 269/2B, First Floor, 'Irai Arul', Vimalraj Street, Nethaji Nagar, Alapakkam Main Road, Maduravoyal, Chennai 600095

ISBN: 9789371975148

10 9 8 7 6 5 4 3 2 1

Book design by Mukul Chand

Printed at Nutech Print Services, India

Contents

Day Three
Deepavali—Night of a Thousand Lamps

Day Four
Govardhan Puja—Lifting Mountains

Day Five
Bhai Dooj—Building Bonds

Legends Beyond Diwali

From Dussehra to Diwali

As the Rajdhani Express rolled into the bustling Howrah Station, Mishti and Rahul peeked through the window, eager to get down.

Soon, they were navigating through Kolkata's busy traffic, packed with Diwali shoppers. The road was dotted with roadside stalls glittering with fairy lights and vendors selling marigold garlands and clay diyas.

'Wow! We need to shop too,' Mishti whispered.

'Yes, I really wanted to take some sondesh, rasgullas and nolen gur delicacies for Nana and Nani, but look at the long queue!' said Mumma.

'It's okay,' said Papa with a chuckle. 'We can come early tomorrow and buy sweets. Right now, the kids are just excited to get home.'

'Yes!' said Rahul, almost bouncing on the seat. 'I'm dying to see if Nani made my favourite shakkarparas!'

The holidays were finally here. Diwali was only six days away and they were at their Nana-Nani's home.

Finally, the taxi stopped and they all jumped out in excitement. The gate was decked up, and the sweet scent of fresh ghee laddoos greeted them as they stepped inside. Nana stood on a stool hanging marigold garlands across the verandah, while Nani gently wiped each clay diya and set it out to dry.

Mumma and Papa hurried to touch Nana and Nani's feet. Mishti flung herself into Nani's arms, while Rahul, drawn by the aroma of frying shakkarparas, dashed straight to the kitchen before hugging Nani tightly.

Nana got down and hugged them all and announced that he still has some cleaning to do before he can go to the market to fetch things for the first day of Diwali.

'Now that we're here, Nana, we'll help with the chores,' said Mishti.

By afternoon the house was sparkling and ready.

Nana patted Rahul's head. 'We missed you during Ramleela and Ravana-dahan this time.'

Papa joined in with the gifts they had brought for Nana and Nani. 'Dussehra and Diwali are two parts of one big story, Rahul,' he said.

'Dussehra is when Lord Ram defeated the ten-headed Ravana and freed Sita Ma. Diwali is the day they returned home to Ayodhya and people lit thousands of lamps to welcome them.'

'Oh, Papa, I am so curious! How come Ravana had ten heads?'

Papa smiled. 'That's quite a story, Rahul. And I'll tell you the story, if you promise to help me put up these Diwali lights later.'

'Can I help you too, Papa?' asked Mishti. Papa laughed. 'Of course! The more, the merrier.'

The Fall of the Ten-Headed Ravana

Legends say that Ravana's father Vishrava was a Brahmin and son of great Sage Pulasttsya. He had married a Rakshasi named Kaikeshi. Together they dreamed of having powerful children—ones who could rule the world some day!

When Kaikesi was about to give birth to her first son, strange and terrifying omens filled the air. Vultures started circling over their home. As the moment of birth approached, the howls of jackals echoed through the trees, dogs started to cry, the earth shook, clouds exploded and the wind blew madly.

Kaikesi felt her heart tremble.

In fear and distress, she gave birth to a baby with ten heads and twenty strong arms, golden hair and sharp teeth.

His body shone like black diamond, dark and dazzling. They named him Dashgreeva, and he grew up to be Ravana.

Then was born the powerful Kumbhakaran, who had a towering body like no one else. Then came the big-faced Surpnakha and then the last son, Vibhishana.

As Ravana grew, so did his desire for power.

He did tapasya for ten thousand years, and every thousand years he offered one of his head to Agni Dev. When he was about to offer his last head, Lord Brahma appeared and stopped him in time.

'I am extremely happy with your perseverance Ravana,' said Brahma. 'Tell me, what do you desire.'

'I want to be invincible. Death should not be able to touch me. No gods, demons, celestial beings, serpents or wild beasts shall ever be able to kill me,' said Ravana proudly.

Lord Brahma smiled and granted Ravana the boon.

But in his pride, Ravana had forgotten to mention humans and monkeys.

And that's how Lord Rama, a human prince, defeated him with the help of the monkey army.

It is this victory of good over evil that we celebrate as Dussehra.

AS PAPA BROUGHT HIS STORY TO AN END, NANI brought chilled lassi drink for everyone.

'Whoa! I love the delicious malai in the lassi, Nani,' Mishti licked her lips as she spoke.

'This creamy goodness makes me think of a very special cow whose milk was truly a gift from god,' said Mumma.

'Which cow?' Curious, Nana asked.

'Kamdhenu, the divine cow, and her daughter Nandini,' said Mumma

'Seems like there are stories even I haven't heard!' said Nana, smiling.

Mumma continued, 'As we all know, cows are considered satwik in Hindu culture. Not only do they provide milk, their dung is used as field manure. And the bulls they give birth to help farmers plough fields and harvest paddy. Cows serve humans in so many ways.

'The twelfth day of the of the Kartik month is celebrated as the Govatsa Dwadashi, also known as Nandini Vrat. In many parts of India, it's like the beginning of Diwali. This unique festival is dedicated to thanking and worshipping the cows and calves for helping us in so many ways.'

'That's interesting! Tell me, Mumma, who was Nandini?' Mishti asked eagerly.

Mumma smiled, and began with the story ...

The Divine Cow Nandini

King Kaushika was returning after winning a battle. On his way back, he happened to pass through Sage Vashistha's hermitage and decided to pay a visit to the great sage.

As he walked into the hermitage, King Kaushika was enchanted by the serenity and abundance of the place. The trees were laden with juicy fruits, and the garden was full of blossoming flowers.

When King Kaushika saw Sage Vashistha, he bowed down to him, but his eyes wandered around the serene surrounding. Kaushika was quite eager to know how one could have so much calmness outside as well as inside.

Sage Vashistha, who had welcomed the king with folded hands, offered him a seat under a large banyan tree. 'Welcome, O King, you are our guest today. Please allow us the honour to serve you and your army,' he said.

Hearing this, Kaushika let out a little laugh. 'I am sure, O Mahatma, you have no idea of the great army I have. There are thousands of foot soldiers, elephants, horses and many more. You live in this forest. How can you possibly offer to feed an entire army of mine?'

Sage Vashistha smiled gently, unfazed by the king's words.

'Do not worry, O King,' the sage said, with calm assurance. 'I think everybody would be very hungry after your long journey. It is our dharma to feed the hungry. Do accept our humble invitation for lunch.

King Kaushika, amused but curious, agreed. 'Let us see how a forest-dwelling hermit feeds a whole army,' he whispered to his commander.

Vashistha then went inside and called upon the divine cow, Nandini, the daughter of Kamadhenu. 'O Nandini, noble one, bless our guests with a meal that fills their hearts and bellies,' he said to her, softly.

At once, the atmosphere of the hermitage changed and fragrance of delicious food filled the air.

Before the eyes of the astonished king emerged platters and vessels filled with fragrant rice, soft rotis, steaming sabzi, sweet laddoos and fruits freshly gathered.

Soldiers who had expected wild fruits and roots were served like royalty. Everyone ate to their heart's content and more.

King Kaushika was stunned.

Now he wanted to know the secret behind this miracle.

'It's all thanks to Nandini,' the sage said. 'She is the daughter of Kamadhenu, the wish-fulfilling cow of the heavens. She lives in our hermitage by divine grace, and she provides whatever is needed joyfully, but only for those who live in dharma.'

A desire to possess Nandini had begun growing in Kaushika's heart. The more he looked at the cow and thought of what she could do, the stronger the fire to have her burnt in him.

'O Rishi, this divine cow would better serve my kingdom,' he said with great politeness. 'Let me take her with me. I will treat her with honour and keep her in the royal palace.'

Vashistha looked into the king's eyes, calm and steady.

'She is not mine to give, O King, nor yours to take. It's Nandini's choice.'

But the king's arrogance blinded him, and he couldn't take no for an answer.

He tried to forcibly take away Nandini.

But as soon he touched her, she roared with a thunderous sound. From her breath came out thousands of warriors, clad in shining armour. From her hooves sprang chariots. From her tail came elephants. From her cry came weapons of fire.

They started destroying Kaushika's army. The soldiers fled, chariots crumbled and elephants fell on the ground.

Later, the grand army created by Nandini merged into her body and disappeared as smoothly as it had appeared.

The mighty king who had returned victorious from a battle stood defeated by a cow.

Just as the story ended, Nani said it was time for lunch. 'Let's all wash our hands and gather at the table,' she said.

'Now I remember Kamdhenu. This divine cow finds mention in many Hindu scriptures. She is believed to have emerged from the churning of the ocean by the gods and demons. Didn't know that her daughter, Nandini, was equally powerful and divine,' said Nana.

The festive lunch table was decorated with fragrant jasmine flowers, their scent blending with the rich aroma of steaming food.

Nani and Mumma were like whirlwind in the kitchen. Every few minutes, one would emerge with a new dish, puffed hot puris, fragrant pulao, crisp aloo tikkis, creamy paneer and bowls of tangy chutneys.

The dining table was laid out with fragrant delicacies and more savouries than Mishti and Rahul could count. Jalebis, barfis, laddoos and the children's favourite, Nani's special besan laddoos.

Looking at so many dishes, Nana chuckled and said, 'Arre, you're bringing out treasures one after another—just like they came from the great Sagar Manthan!'

'What's Sagar Manthan, Nana?' asked Mishti.

'O, it's a great story about a magical ocean,' Nana replied. 'It's my turn to tell a story, I guess'

Day One

Dhanteras—Treasures of the Deep

Churning the Ocean (Samudra Manthan)

IT WAS A LONG TIME AGO, DURING A GRAND CELEBRATION in the heavens.

Everyone had devoured a big feast, and were swaying to the celestial music being played by the Gandharvas.

Sura, the divine liquor, was flowing freely and the air smelt of sweet sandalwood and blooming lotuses.

Everyone was in a joyful mood and had let their guards down. With their senses blurred by sura, the laughter of the Devas echoed through the heavenly halls.

Indra, the king of Devas, was at the centre of it all. He was riding on his divine white elephant, while the apsaras danced in his honour.

Indra, pleased with so much admiration and honour, was carried away by a sudden feeling of arrogance.

As he strutted through the heavens, he bumped into Sage Durvasa, known for his fiery temper and unpredictable curses.

But that day, seeing the handsome Indra being honoured with music and flower showers, Durvasa was in a rare mood of kindness.

He smiled, then took off from around his neck a divine garland made of magical flowers. It was a garland that had been blessed by Sri, the goddess of wealth. Durvasa gifted it to Indra.

But Indra, in his infinite wisdom (or lack thereof), thought it would be a great idea to put the garland onto his elephant's trunk instead of wearing it himself.

The poor elephant was overwhelmed by the strong fragrance of the flowers, which had also attracted many bees. As the bees buzzed around his trunk, the mighty elephant swung his head this way and that, to relieve himself.

Annoyed and uncomfortable, the elephant finally decided he had had enough. With one loud trumpet, he flung the lovely garland to the ground. Then, accidentally, he trampled it to bits under his giant feet.

Everyone was shocked, but none more than Sage Durvasa.

His eyes widened and his face turned red. He clenched his teeth and shouted, 'This garland was a blessing from the goddess Sri. You dared to insult a divine gift?'

The cloud of pride lifted and Indra came back to his senses. By the time he realised what had happened, it was too late.

Sage Durvasa's voice echoed through the heavens, 'You, Indra, and all the Devas, shall lose all your powers, your wealth and your glow. From this moment on, darkness will envelop the lands!'

Saying this, Durvasa walked away from the heavens.

Soon goddess Sri quietly left the heavens. No one noticed at first. But slowly, everything began to change. The flowers stopped blooming and the music faded. The surroundings became pale and dusty, and everyone started feeling weak and tired.

The heaven fell into a shroud of darkness, which penetrated the hearts of the mighty Devas too, leaving them frail and broken.

Asuras, who always looked for an opportunity to strike, found it an inviting one. They attacked the heavens with full force, defeating the Devas and banishing them from their own home.

With broken hearts and spirits, the Devas went to Brahma for help.

'O father of the worlds,' Indra pleaded, 'we have been driven out of our own homes. We were foolish, and we were punished. What shall we do now?'

Brahma listened with a calm gaze. After a brief pause, he spoke.

'Pride led you astray, and humility has brought you to me. But only Lord Vishnu can help restore balance now.

Let's go to him. His wisdom holds the key to the prosperity of the earth and heavens.'

The Devas soon reached Vaikuntha with their heads bowed and theirs hands folded.

Lord Vishnu was lying calmly on the Sheshnag, floating on the ocean that was as white as milk.

'Save us, O Narayan, everything we ever owned has been usurped by the cunning Asuras. We have lost all powers and we feel helpless,' pleaded the Devas.

'Now, whatever has been done cannot be undone,' said Lord Vishnu. 'There is only one way to get back all the power and strength. That is to fetch amrit, the elixir of immortality, present at the depths of the ocean. You must churn the Ksheer Sagara, the ocean of milk.'

But churning the vast ocean as infinite as the Ksheer Sagara was no easy task, and the Devas were already very weak. They turned to Lord Vishnu and asked, 'How can anyone churn an ocean?'

'Become friends with the Asuras,' he said. 'They are strong. Take their help. Work together, as this churning will require the might of both divine and demonic forces. Only in unity can the impossible become possible.'

The Devas exchanged glances. Friendship with Asuras? The very beings who drove us away from our homes?

'Yes,' said Vishnu.

Though Indra was hesitant and unsure, he knew there was no other way. Swallowing his pride, he journeyed to the dark, fiery realms of Patal Lok and stood before Bali, the king of the Asuras.

'It's the nectar of immortality, and you shall have your share,' said Indra to Bali.

Between suspicion and the promise of eternal life, the Asuras argued and debated. Finally, they agreed to the mammoth task.

A pact was made. The Devas and Asuras came together, and dragged the mighty Mandara mountain through forests and valleys, into the Ksheer Sagara.

But for the churning to begin, they needed a rope.

And so, they turned to Vasuki, the majestic king of serpents, who coiled around the mountain.

The Asuras, filled with pride, shouted, 'We will not hold the tail, which is the dirty end. We will hold the head. A serpent's head is royal and we deserve it!'

The Devas, humbled by their defeat at the hands of the Asuras, quietly took the tail end. And the churning began.

Soon Mandara mountain started slipping into the waters and sank to the depths of the ocean.

That's when Lord Vishnu took the form of a giant Kurma, a turtle. He held the mountain on his back, so the churning wouldn't stop.'

The Devas and the Asuras churned and churned, and then a terrible thing started happening.

From the depths of the ocean, deadly dark fumes began to rise. They were thick and suffocating. It was Halahala, the most poisonous venom in the universe.

Vasuki, being used as the churning rope, was writhing in pain by now. The friction had made him breathless. The dark fumes rising from the ocean made even more venom spill from his open jaws.

'The poison! The poison is killing everything!' shouted the Asuras, covering their faces. A wave of panic spread. Many Asuras and Devas started choking and fell unconscious.

Far away on snow-laden Mount Kailash, Lord Shiva sat deep in samadhi, untouched by time. But the cries of pain reached him, even in his stillness. His eyes opened slowly. The compassionate lord had heard the suffering of the world.

Rising from his meditation, Shiva stepped forward, his matted hair swaying and his trident gleaming with light. He looked at the fear in the hearts of gods and demons alike.

Without a moment's hesitation, he cupped the deadly Halahala poison in his divine hand and drank it like it was water.

He drank it all to protect the world, holding it in his throat, not allowing it to reach his stomach. His throat turned intense blue, and he became Neelkantha, the blue-throated one.

When Goddess Lakshmi Emerged

WITH THE POISON SWALLOWED AND THE WORLD SAFE once again, the churning continued. The mountain turned, and then something shimmered beneath the waters.

From the depths of the ocean, the first divine gift arose—Kamdhenu, the celestial cow with a body as white as moonlight. It had the power to fulfil any wish you made.

One by one, the ocean started giving birth to celestial beings and objects—the wish-fulfilling tree Kalpavriksha, Kaustubha gem, Chandra the moon, elephant Airavat, the magical white horse Uchchaihshravas and so many more.

One after another, 14 divine treasures, known as the Ratnas, rose from the depths of the ocean.

And then, with a blazing golden brightness that blinded everyone, emerged Sri Lakshmi, the goddess of wealth, beauty and fortune. Her eyes filled with compassion and her palms overflowing with abundance, all the Devas bowed to her in reverence.

Sri Lakshmi walked past the gods and demons, smiling at each of them. Then she turned her gaze lovingly to Lord Vishnu, who stood calm and timeless. She went ahead and placed a garland around his neck, choosing him as her eternal companion.

This divine wedding is celebrated as Lakshmi Puja, on the first day of Diwali. But in many parts of India, this puja is observed on the third day of Diwali.

It's also said that in love and honour of Sri Lakshmi, Lord Vishnu got a sacred mark (a sort of tattoo) on his chest. This mark, called the 'srivatsa', depicts his inseparable bond with his partner.

Finally, the day they had all been waiting for arrived. After all the toil, a golden kalasha rose above the waves, held in the powerful hands of Dhanvantari, the divine physician. His robust body and blue-coloured skin looked radiant clad in yellow silk. In the kalasha held by him was the Amrit.

Once the nectar was out, it triggered a fight between the Devas and the Asuras. The fragile peace between them began to crack.

The Asuras shouted, 'The Amrit is ours! We deserve it first!'

One of the Asuras moved briskly, snatched the pot and ran away. There was a big argument who would drink it first.

Lord Vishnu smiled. He then took the form of a divine maiden, Mohini, and tricked the Asuras.

'Let me distribute it,' said Mohini. 'I promise to give everyone their rightful share.'

The Asuras, charmed by her beauty, sat in a queue, waiting for their turn. One by one, Mohini walked past the Devas and poured the Amrit into their cups, and skipped the Asuras.

One clever Asura named Swarbhanu noticed what was going on. He quietly slipped into the queue of Devas.

Just as he was about to drink the nectar, Surya and Chandra spotted him.

'He is not one of us!' they screamed.

In an instant, Vishnu hurled his Sudarshan Chakra, slicing off Swarbhanu's head before the nectar passed his throat. But a few drops had already touched his lips. And so, his head and his body became immortal. The head came to be known as Rahu, and the body as Ketu.

Both the good and the evil reside within each of of us. The story of sagar manthan is a story of our mind which, when churned, reveals positive and negative traits of ours. First, poison is ejected, then some good stuff like treasures, some superpowers and finally the amrit is revealed.

'WOW! THIS IS SUCH AN AWESOME STORY. A MAGICAL ocean and so many treasures that came out of it. Thank you, Nana!' said Rahul, his eyes wide with wonder. 'Also, Dhanvantari and Dhanteras sounds similiar. Is that why we celebrate the first day of Diwali in honour of him, Nana?'

'Ah, you noticed that, Rahul! Yes, you're absolutely right,' said Nana. 'The name Dhanteras is derived from two words: dhan, which means wealth, and teras, which translates to thirteenth. Dhanteras is celebrated on the thirteenth lunar day of the month of Kartik in the Hindu calendar.

'And who better to honour on this day than Lord Dhanvantari, the divine physician. He brought not just wealth, but the greatest treasure of all—good health and long life.'

'Let me add here,' said Papa, 'that Lord Vishnu had predicted he would be born as human in his Dhanvantri avatar to spread the knowledge of Ayurveda and medicine. Let me tell you about this legend.'

The Birth of Dhanvantari

In the ancient tower of Kashi lived a noble King, Dirghatamas. He ruled with great love and care for his people, treating them like his own family.

But his people were going through hard and challenging times.

A deadly epidemic had spread rapidly through the country. It weakened the body and spirit of his people. There were no proper medicines, no real doctors, and the people of his kingdom suffered in pain.

King Dirghatamas couldn't bear to watch his people in such agony. So he left the palace, and walked barefoot into the forest. He sat under an old Banyan tree and began to pray.

Days turned into weeks, and weeks into months. He ate very little, and spoke to no one. With folded hands and a heart full of faith, he called out to Lord Dhanvantari, the

divine healer who had once emerged from the ocean with the nectar of immortality.

'O Lord, this world needs a healer,' he pleaded. 'I do not ask for name or fame. I pray to you to take birth as my son, so that you may bring the boon of healing to this earth.'

And then, in a vision of golden light, Lord Dhanvantari appeared, calm and radiant.

'Your wish is selfless, King Dirghatamas,' he said. 'You asked not for yourself, but for the world. For that reason, I shall take birth as your son.'

Soon after, Lord Dhanvantari was born in the royal household of Kashi.

Even as a young boy, he showed signs of spiritual wisdom. Once he grew up, he shared his divine knowledge of Ayurveda, teaching it to sages and rishis, who became his devoted disciples.

The day of his birth is celebrated as Dhanvantari Jayanti, which also falls on Dhanteras.

Just as Papa finished the story, he stood up with a smile.

'Okay then,' he said, 'Nana and I need to head to the market to buy a silver coin and a few more things for the evening puja.'

At once, Rahul sat up. 'Papa, can I, too, come with you to the market?' he asked eagerly.

'Sure, Rahul,' said Nana. 'But be ready for the crowds and heat as during the Diwali season, the markets turn into a madhouse, with sales, bargains and discounts flying everywhere!'

As they began putting on their shoes, Nana continued, 'You see, Rahul, Diwali isn't just about lights and sweets. It is closely linked to commerce too. The first day of the festival, Dhanteras, is also about celebrating wealth. It is believed that Sri Lakshmi emerged from the mighty ocean on this very auspicious day.

In the market, Rahul was intrigued to see people swarming the shops, eager to buy gold, silver, precious stones and even kitchen utensils. It was all in the belief that such shiny treasures will attract Goddess Lakshmi into their homes.

After hours of shopping and navigating through crowded lanes, picking up flower garlands, fresh flowers, a silver coin and even a new broom, Rahul's feet began to drag and he let out a sigh.

'Papa, can we go home now?'

Nana, balancing a bag of diyas, smiled gently.

'Yes, let's go back. We still have to get ready for the evening puja, light the diyas and welcome Lakshmi into our home.'

Once home, Rahul watched Nani put oil in the clay diyas. She asked the kids to place them all around the house—at the entrance, balconies, windows, parking, near garbage cans and one at the holy tulsi plant.

'Those lamps are called Yama Deep,' said Nani to the children. 'Yama is the lord of death. On Dhanteras, people please him and pray to him for the long lives of their family and loved ones. For this reason, Dhanteras is also known as Yamadeepdaan.'

'Quickly put all the diyas in place and come back. I will tell you an interesting legend about Yama Deep.

Did you know, there is a unique practice of buying brooms on Dhanteras? Bringing a broom home on this auspicious day symbolises the sweeping away of debt and the act of inviting Goddess Lakshmi to take up residence in one's home.

Mishti hurriedly placed all the little clay lamps and came running, a little out of breath. 'All done, Nani! Now tell us the story.'

Ashtalakshmi is a group of the eight manifestations of Devi Lakshmi.

- Maha Lakshmi — Primeval form of Lakshmi that appeared during the milking of the oceans
- Dhana Lakshmi — Giver of material wealth
- Dhanya Lakshmi — Associated with food, grains and agricultural wealth
- Gaja Lakshmi — Bestows animal wealth
- Santan Lakshmi — Bestows offspring and children
- Dhairya Lakshmi — Blesses with courage and patience
- Vijaya Lakshmi — Blesses with success
- Vidya Lakshmi — Bestows knowledge

'Children,' Nani said, placing the last diya near the back wall, 'people celebrate Yama Deep or Yamadeepdaan on Dhanteras by lighting oil lamps outside their homes. It's our way of praying for the well-being and long life of our loved ones and keeping misfortune away.'

Just then, Nana stepped out with the aarti thali, Rahul came running with a box of matches, and they all sang aarti in praise of Lord Dhanvantari and Sri Lakshmi.

King Hima and the Soothsayer

THERE WAS A GREAT KING NAMED HIMA. HE HAD A SON whom the king doted upon.

The little boy's playfulness and charm were a source of great happiness for the king. He had great plans for the little boy's future.

One day, a well-known soothsayer who was visiting the kingdom came to the king's court. On seeing the toddler and reading his birthchart, he predicted an untimely death for the little prince.

'With a heart full of remorse and my apologies, Maharaj, but the charts say that our prince would be bitten by a poisonous snake and would die on the fourth day of his marriage.'

King Hima couldn't believe what he had heard. He was heartbroken and inconsolable. He tried all kinds of prayers, rituals and pilgrimage asking for the boy's long life.

Many such years of yearning passed, and despite the prediction the prince was married at the age of sixteen. The new bride soon heard of the soothsayer's forecast and was worried. But she was determined to save her husband from the clutches of death.

Three days after the marriage, anxiety set in, and the fourth night was a sleepless one. The couple laid awake to the slightest of movement and sound. The new bride took all her gold ornaments, silver coins and gifts, and placed them on the entrance of her bedroom.

Inside the room, she hid her husband behind her. She had lit hundreds of oil lamps, which were put at every corner of the house.

All night long, she sat at the door, loudly narrating stories, singing melodious songs and keeping the lamps burning bright, as if to say, 'Yamraj, I will not let you pass!'

Meanwhile, Yamraj came in the form of a black snake. But as he wriggled along, he was blinded by the dazzling jewellery and the hundreds of lamps flickering around him.

He crawled on top of the mountain of treasures, captivated by the bride's melodious songs, and sat listening to her all night long.

As dawn approached, Lord Yamaraj slithered away without doing any harm to the prince.

Thanks to his wife's quick thinking, the prince's life was saved.

Day Two

Chhoti Diwali—Lights Before the Dawn

As the evening came to a close, Mishti and Rahul sat besides Nani. Their eyes were tired but hearts full of excitement. They wanted to fall asleep quickly, for their cousins were arriving early morning on Choti Diwali.

'Nani,' Rahul asked sleepily, 'why do we have Choti Diwali before the real Diwali?'

Nani smiled and said, 'Ah, my little one, Choti Diwali is like the beginning of the big celebration of Diwali. It is celebrated in different parts of India and is known by many names such as Bhoot Chaturdashi, Narak Chaudas, Roop Chaudas, Choti Diwali, Narak Nivaran Chaturdashi and Kali Chaudas. It's also called Naraka Chaturdashi; it's the day Lord Krishna defeated the cruel demon Narakasura.'

Mishti sat up a little. 'Was he very bad?'

'Very bad,' Nani nodded. 'Let me tell you how he was slain,' she said.

The Slaying of Narakasura

Narakasura was born from Lord Vishnu and Bhudevi, the earth goddess. As he grew older, he became cruel and arrogant. He started keeping bad company, especially with the demon Banasura. He strayed from his righteous path and slowly, he forgot what was good and what was evil.

He ruled the lands of Pragjyotishyapur and terrorised everyone with his presence.

He craved for more and more power and wanted to become invincible. So he did a severe penance and called Brahma. When Brahma appeared, Narakasura asked for a interesting boon—that no one in the universe could kill him, except his own mother.

Brahma granted the wish and Narakasura became even more arrogant. 'Who would ever hurt their own child?' he thought. But he didn't know that his mother was Bhudevi, the gentle, patient Mother Earth herself.

When her own son began hurting innocent people, she couldn't stay silent. To restore balance and end his cruelty, she took birth as Satyabhama, who went on to become Krishna's queen.

Meanwhile, with many boons and growing confidence, Narakasura's cruelty had only increased. He would torment innocent people without mercy. His hunger for power knew no limits and he now had started troubling the Devas too.

To take control of the elements, Narakasura stole Varuna's umbrella, which was a symbol of the sea god's dominion over cosmic order. He also stole the divine earrings of Aditi, the revered mother of the gods.

Day by day, Narakasura became infamous for abducting women, especially the daughters of Devas and noble families, locking them away in his palace like they were trophies.

One day, Aditi came weeping to Satyabhama and told her about the cruel acts of Narakasura. 'Narakasura has stolen my earrings,' she sobbed. 'He has also imprisoned thousands of innocent princesses. No one dares to stop him.'

Satyabhama's eyes filled with resolve. She turned to Krishna and said firmly, 'This must end.'

Krishna nodded. 'It is time to free the world from Narakasura.'

Krishna and Satyabhama decided to put an end to the long ongoing saga of tyranny and injustice. They mounted the powerful Garuda and flew to the kingdom of Pragjyotishyapur.

On seeing the couple arrive, Narakasura sent his powerful general, Mura. 'Go, kill them now!' he roared. Mura entered the battle scene with his huge demon army, but Krishna vanquished all of them effortlessly.

Wielding his divine weapons, Krishna decimated many of Narakasura's soldiers. His prowess and skill in battle struck fear into the hearts of the demon army. Narakasura took his powerful trident and hurled it towards Krishna. The blazing trident hit Krishna on his chest, causing him to faint.

Satyabhama was distraught to see her husband unconscious. Fuming with anger, she picked up Krishna's weapon and shot a divine arrow at the demon king. The fire-emitting arrow hit its target and pierced Narakasura's chest. He fell with an agonising cry.

Krishna freed the 16,000 women who had been imprisoned by Narakasura and married them.

Before dying, Narakasura asked his mother, Bhudevi, for a boon. He wished for his death not to be mourned but celebrated with lights and colours, symbolising the triumph of good over evil.

Thus the tradition of celebrating Diwali as Naraka Chaturdashi was born, especially in South India, where people light up their homes in joyous festivities.

Rahul whispered, 'Wow! Truth wins!' His eyes sparkled with joy, making Nani smile. 'Always, beta. It may take time, but light always finds its way,' she said.

'Nani, what's the fun part of Choti Diwali, apart from prayers and all the cleaning,' Rahul asked.

Nani chuckled. 'There's more fun than you think!'

'Like what?' Mishti perked up.

Nani began, 'There's a very interesting tradition related to Naraka Chaturdashi. In some parts of India, people take a bitter fruit, like bitter gourd, and smash it under their foot.'

'Eww! Why?' asked Rahul.

'It's symbolic of crushing evil underfoot!' Nani said with a twinkle in her eye. 'It shows Krishna's victory over Narakasura. Some people even taste a drop of the bitter juice, which they say represents the demon's blood.'

'Gross!' laughed Mishti. 'But it's also kind of cool.'

Nani leaned in playfully. 'I don't want to scare you, but did you know tomorrow is like India's very own Halloween?'

'What!' both kids shouted.

'Yes,' Nani nodded. 'In our Bengal, it's called Bhoot Chaturdashi, the night of spirits. My friend from college told me all about it.

'Tell us too, Nani,' Mishti requested.

'Alright ...' said Nani.

Bhoot refers to something that has existed in the past, and is often associated with ghosts. Chaturdashi means the fourteenth day. Bhoot Chaturdashi is celebrated on the fourteenth day of Krishna Paksha in the month of Kartik. It is believed to be the time when the living and the dead come closest.

Our forefathers designed and planned our festivals according to seasons, harvests and our needs. According to the Charaka Samhita, this time of the year marks the end of the monsoon season and the onset of winter, traditionally one of the harshest seasons to endure. During this period, incorporating green leafy vegetables and herbs in our diet is a good way to boost immunity.

Ghosts of Bhoot Chaturdashi

THERE WAS A LAZY BRAHMIN COUPLE WHO NEVER cleaned their house. It used to be dirty all the time. Trash piled up in every corner of their home, and dark forces started living in those unclean places.

The couple started falling sick often. Day by day, they also started losing their mental peace, and would often go without taking baths or cleaning up.

One day, a ghost popped out of the garbage—and then one more and another and then yet another.

The next day, the brahmin and his wife cleaned every corner of their home, and sprinkled water infused with fourteen kinds of leafy greens around the house. That's how Bhoot Chaturdashi began, as a way to purify the homes and keep spirits away.

'AS SPOOKY AS THE NAME SOUNDS, IT'S ALSO A VERY special day. It's believed that on Bhoot Chaturdashi, a portal opens between our world and the spirit world,' said Nani.

'Like a magic door?' Mishti whispered.

'Nani nodded, as the kids huddled, excited and a bit spooked, 'Our ancestors—fourteen generations of them—come down to visit us. We light fourteen diyas around the house, to guide them home.'

'Some say, long ago, bad tantriks would try scary things the night before Kali Puja,' Nani whispered. 'So families kept their children safe at home, fed them food made with leafy greens and lit up every corner.'

She continued, 'In Bengal, people specially cook Choddo Shaak with fourteen types of leafy greens like mustard, neem, fenugreek, dill, coriander, drumstick leaves, beet greens and more. It's a celebration of the magic hidden in seasonal greens.'

Mishti whispered, 'It's like a festival of lights, lots of good food and now ghosts?'

Nani smiled, tucking them in. 'Call it what you like, Chhoti Diwali, Naraka Chaturdashi, Kali Chaudas or Bhoot Chaturdashi, but it's really a day to clean your space, light up your heart, eat nourishing food and remember those who came before us.'

Mishti yawned, 'I'd like to know more, Nani,' she said. 'But I'm feeling sleepy.'

Rahul mumbled, 'I'm sleepy too, but don't forget to tell us more tomorrow.'

Nani smiled, kissed their foreheads and whispered, 'I promise. Now, have a good night sleep and wake up early for the Abhyanga Snan.'

The next morning, Nana came to the room and shook Rahul and Mishti awake. 'Time to get up. Your cousin Keshu is here,' he whispered.

Yawning loudly and stretching their arms, the children jumped out of bed to meet their cousin who had just arrived from Mumbai. Keshu had come bearing sweets and toys. They all giggled and came to the verandah, where Nani was waiting with a bowl of fragrant, warm herbal oil.

One by one, she gently massaged all the children with the oil.

Then, they all took bath and changed into new clothes.

'Hurry now!' Nani said, picking up the sweet boxes and flowers in her carry bag. 'We must reach the temple of our Kula Devta in time!'

Choddo Shaak
Diwali Special Bengali Recipe
Ingradients :-
Spinach
Fenugreek Leaves
Neem Leaves
Dill Leaves
Beetroot Leaves
Method :- 1)
1) Marinate Brinjal in ½ tspn of turmeric
Chop the Brinjal in fine cubes.
2) In a saucepan, add mustard oil and mustard seeds
3) Then add brinjal cubes and add green vegetables
SA
P
4) Let the vegetables cook until you can eat.

'Kula Devta?' Mishti asked, curious. 'What does that mean, Nani?'

'Kula Devta is the guardian deity of a family line,' Nani explained as they got into the car. 'He protects the family through generations. For our family, it is Lord Hanuman.'

Mishti looked confused. 'Nani, I always thought Diwali was a lot about Lord Ram. It is the day he came back to Ayodhya after defeating Ravana, isn't it?'

'Yes, you are right, my dear,' Nani smiled. 'But before Rama returns, it was Hanuman who helped build the bridge to Lanka. He is the one who found Sita, set fire to Lanka and stood by Ram when he felt weak. Without Hanuman, the victory wouldn't have been complete.'

Rahul's eyes widened. 'So Hanuman was like a hero behind the scenes?'

'Exactly!' Nani nodded. 'That's why many families like ours first bow to Hanuman on Choti Diwali, to seek his blessings. Only then do we celebrate the return of Lord Rama.'

Then Nani said something that stumped the kids. 'Do you know some say that Hanuman was like Rama's brother?'

'Wow, that's something new!' Mishti exclaimed.

Nani smiled. 'Yes, but I have heard many versions of this story. Let me tell you one ...'

Why is Hanuman Worshipped Before Lord Ram?

ONCE, IN A DENSE FOREST, A KIND WOMAN NAMED Anjana called upon Lord Shiva, praying deeply for a child.

Meanwhile, in the kingdom of Ayodhya, King Dasharatha was performing a holy ritual called the Putrakameshti Yagna to have children of his own.

With the blessings of Lord Vishnu, King Dasharatha received a pot of divine prasad, which he was instructed to share with his three queens. As they were partaking the delicious prasad, an eagle dived down and took a small portion of the pudding. It then flew over the forest where Anjana was meditating.

Vayu, the god of wind, gently guided the pudding into Anjana's hands after the eagle dropped it by some divine coincidence.

Feeling grateful for this unexpected prasad, Anjana ate the pudding. After some time, she gave birth to Hanuman, the fearless monkey god who would grow up to be an ardent devotee of Lord Rama.

It was at Rishimukh Mountain that Hanuman first met Lord Rama. The lord and Lakshmana had come there looking for Sita, who had been abducted by the demon king Ravana.

From the very first moment, Hanuman's heart was filled with deep devotion for Rama. He bowed with folded hands and declared, 'I am your servant forever. I will find Sita and bring her back to you.'

Hanuman crossed the mighty ocean in a single bound, reached the golden city of Lanka. He searched far and wide until he found Sita in Ashok Vatika, sitting under a tree, sorrowful but strong.

Hanuman gave her Rama's message: 'He is coming for you, Mata. Do not lose hope.'

Hanuman's unwavering loyalty and bravery helped Rama defeat Ravana and destroy Lanka, bringing ma Sita back safely.

In recognition of Hanuman's selfless service and unwavering faith, Rama blessed him with immortality. 'O Hanuman, you will live as long as my name is spoken on earth,' he declared. 'Those who seek me, must first seek you.'

'And that is why we pray to Lord Hanuman on Choti Diwali,' said Nani.

At the temple, offerings were lovingly made to Lord Hanuman—his favorite laddoos, fresh paan, fragrant kevda perfume and beautiful rose garlands. And then, everyone in the family prayed for his blessings and protection.

As the sun began to set, they returned home. The house glowed gently in the light of ghee lamps as everyone gathered to enjoy a majestic feast.

After dinner, Mishti and Rahul rushed out to the terrace, where Papa was already lighting the first sparkler.

Papa handed a glowing sparkler to Mishti, who squealed with delight.

'Hold it carefully!' Papa said with a smile, lighting another for Rahul.

They whirled their sparklers in wide circles, laughing and running about as golden sparks danced in the air around them.

Day Three

Deepavali— Night of a Thousand Lamps

As the children settled down for bedtime, little Keshu tugged at Nani's sari and whispered, 'Nani, can you tell us everything about Rama and Sita?'

'Ah, Keshu, it's the most beautiful story. And how lucky I am to be telling you their story, tonight, on the eve of Diwali—the very day they returned home after fourteen long years in exile.'

The children huddled closer as Nani began the story.

Triumphant Return of Lord Rama with Sita

FROM THE SACRED OFFERINGS OF THE YAGNA, FOUR SONS were born to King Dashratha.

Kausalya gave birth to the eldest son, Rama, who is considered to be the avatar of Lord Vishnu. He was born with many divine qualities.

Sumitra had two sons, Lakshmana and Shatrughna, and Kaikeyi gave birth to Bharata.

All four sons of Dashratha had an extraordinary upbringing, and they grew up to be well-mannered, knowledgeable and brave. The three younger brothers, adored their eldest brother, Rama, and so did everyone in the kingdom.

After many years at the gurukul, all four princes got married and settled into marital life. Ram married Sita, the beautiful princess of Mithila.

As the years passed, King Dashratha began to grow old and frail. He decided to crown Rama as the next king of Ayodhya. The news spread fast and brought joy to many people. As preparations for the coronation started, the people of Ayodhya decorated the city. Overjoyed, they broke into music and dance, eagerly anticipating a golden age under Rama's rule.

However, not all were happy with the news, especially not the younger queen, Kaikeyi. While her heart had once been full of love for Rama, Kaikeyi got swayed by her cunning maid, Manthara, who reminded Kaikeyi that the king owed her two boons. Long ago, Kaikeyi had saved Dashratha's life, and he had promised her that he would fulfil two of her wishes, whenever she asked.'

Now, in a moment clouded by fear and jealousy, Kaikeyi asked for her two wishes to be fulfilled.

'For my first boon,' she said, 'let my son Bharat be crowned king of Ayodhya. And for my second boon, I ask that Rama be sent away into exile for fourteen years.'

Kaikeyi's two wishes shattered the king. He loved Rama more than his own life, but a promise was a promise. Rama, noble and obedient, accepted his exile without hesitation.

And his loving wife Sita and loyal brother Lakshmana insisted on going with him.'

While living in exile, Rama killed many demons. Together with Lakshmana, he kept the Dandakaranya forest safe for the sages and ascetics who lived in it.

One day, a demoness named Shurpanakha saw Rama in the forest. Drawn by his charm and personality, she pursued him to marry her. When Ram declined stating that he already had a wife, Shurpanakha went to Lakshmana but he, too, declined her proposal.

Feeling humiliated, Shurpanakha pounced on Sita, but Lakshmana stopped her in time. In a fit of rage, he cut off Shurpanakha's nose and ears.

A bleeding Shurpanakha went to her brother, Ravana, and told him the entire story. She spoke of Sita's beauty and persuaded Ravana to abduct and marry her.

Ravana became obsessed with Sita and he planned to kidnap her. He managed to trick everyone with a magical golden deer, and when both Rama and Lakshmana left their abode, Ravana kidnapped Sita. He took her to Lanka, and when she refused to marry him, he kept her prisoner in Ashok Vatika.

While Ravana forcibly took Sita in Pushpak Vimana, Sita cried for help. She also threw her ornaments on the way, to attract the attention of any passer-by. Her ornaments fell in different parts of forest and faraway lands.

When Rama and Lakshmana returned to find that Sita had been abducted, they were heartbroken. They set off on a long journey to find her and bring her back. While searching for Sita, they met the monkey king Sugreeva, his minister Jambavan and companion Hanuman at Rishimukh Mountain. In the spirit of friendship, Rama helped Sugreeva retrieve his kingdom of Kishkindha. Feeling grateful, Sugreeva promised Rama that he and his monkey army will find and bring back Sita.

Hanuman recognised Rama as the Supreme Lord, and was ready to serve his master in any way. He travelled across the ocean to find Sita.

Hanuman found her at last, in the golden city of Lanka, sitting quietly under a tree in Ashok Vatika. He could see how, despite its beauty, the garden felt like a prison to Sita.

She was surrounded by demonesses who tried every trick to scare her, while the cruel Ravana kept visiting her, repeatedly asking her to marry him. But Sita, brave and unshaken, kept resisting his advances. Her heart only belonged to Rama.

Unable to see mother Sita in so much pain, Hanuman finally went up to Sita and introduced himself as a servant and messenger of Lord Rama. He presented her with Rama's ring so she could trust him, and he gave her Rama's message—that he was coming to get her.

Then he began uprooting the trees and destroying the beautiful garden. Soon he was captured by Ravana's son Indrajeet and the soldiers, and his tail was put on fire, by order of Ravana. Hanuman quickly shrunk his size and began to jump from one building to another.

After burning down the whole of Lanka, he jumped into the ocean. With the fire put out, he returned to Lord Rama. Once there, he narrated the entire story of how Sita was being kept captive by Ravana. Lord Rama listened with tears in his eyes.

Soon, tears gave way to fury, and Rama decided to wage war on Lanka without delay. He summoned Hanuman, Sugreeva, Jambavan and a whole army of monkeys. Together, they traversed through the forests and built Rama Setu, a sea bridge, to reach Lanka.

Rama's army arrived in Lanka, leading to conflicts with Ravana's sons and generals. Ravana's son Indrajeet struck Lakshmana with his Shakti bow, making him unconscious. Hanuman quickly flew to the Himalayas, and brought back the magical herb Sanjivni, saving Lakshmana's life.

A fierce battle broke out between Rama and Ravana. With the aid of the gods, Rama ultimately overpowered Ravana, and put an end to the ten-headed demon king by piercing him with his arrows.

Reunited with Sita and the period of their exile now over, Lord Rama decided to return to Ayodhya. Along with

Sita, Lakshmana and the rest of his followers, he flew home on the Pushpaka Vimana.

Bharat, the younger brother who had become the reason for the fourteen-year exile of his beloved brother, had waited patiently all these years. When the news of his eldest brother's arrival reached his ear, he grew ecstatic with joy and cried in relief.

The city of Ayodhya, which had lost its lustre in the absence of the divine couple, returned to life.

Guru Vasishtha, ministers of court, the three queens of Dashtratha and the people of Ayodhya who had waited for fourteen long years for the arrival of their beloved king Shri Rama were eager to see him return.

They decorated the whole city. The streets, temples, and roads were lined with flowers, rangoli and lamps. All the houses in the city were painted in vibrant colours and decorated.

People climbed atop their houses waiting to catch a glance of Pushpak Viman that was bringing back their beloved Rama and Sita. Women dressed in finery sang their praises.

Since the return of Lord Rama and Sita to Ayodhya was celebrated with countless rows of ghee deepas, the festival came to be known as Deepavali.

'YOU KNOW, CHILDREN, SOME OTHER BEINGS, TOO, celebrate this festival,' said Nani.'Who, Nani?' asked Mishti, with curiosity in her eyes.

Nani lowered her voice, like she was letting them in on a secret. 'Yakshas,' she said. 'They are mythical beings with Lord Kubera, the god of wealth, as their chief. They are thought to be spirits residing in trees, mountains, rivers and oceans. They celebrate a special night called Yaksha Ratri.'

'Yaksha Ratri?' repeated Rahul, trying the strange new word on his tongue.

'Yes! It's a night of joy and gambling,' Nani chuckled.

'Long ago, the Yakshas would gather under the moonlight, throw flower dice and play games. Their king, Kubera, would sit on a throne of gold and watch followers cheer and sing.'

Mishti gasped, 'Is that why people play cards on Diwali night?'

'Ah, now you see,' smiled Nani. 'Some say it began with them. Others believe that the Yakshas gamble on that night to invite luck and prosperity. It's all part of the same magical story!'

Kubera and Yaksha Ratri

KUBERA, THE YAKSHA KING, ONCE UNDERTOOK INTENSE penance to please Brahma. Impressed by his deep devotion, Brahma appeared and granted him incredible boons. Riches beyond imagination, the magical flying chariot Pushpak Viman and the ruling seat of the magnificent golden city of Lanka.

But fate had other plans. His step brother, Ravana, attacked Kubera, seized Lanka and stole the Pushpak Viman, forcing him to flee.

Displaced and humiliated, Kubera made his new home at the foot of Mount Kailash, in Alkapuri, a city as splendid as a dream. Alkapuri was so enchanting, that it rivalled even the celestial home of Indra.

Once, when Lord Shiva and Parvati visited Alkapuri, Kubera saw the couple, and his eyes fell upon Goddess Parvati.

In awe, he was about to close his eyes in reverence, but Parvati misunderstood his gaze as disrespect. Offended by his behaviour, she raised her arms in anger and burst one of his eyes.

Shocked and sorrowful, Kubera begged for forgiveness, explaining he meant no harm.

Touched by his sincere apology, Parvati restored his eye, though it remained smaller than the other. Shiva appointed Kubera as the guardian of the North, and Parvati named him the lord of wealth.

While the goddess creates wealth, Kubera distributes it.

It is believed that on the night of Diwali Yakshas come out of their dwellings, visit villages and homes with bags of money, and play games of dice with people. Those who manage to defeat the Yakshas are believed to receive great bounties.

This is why playing cards on the festival of Diwali is popular. It is believed that gambling on the festival of lights pleases Kubera and earns people his goodwill.

Mishti giggled, 'I am sure Kubera must be very, very rich, Nani. He must have mountains of gold and gems!'

Nani laughed softly, 'Oh yes, child. So much that he can fill rivers with coins and still have plenty left!'

Then Mishti's eyes sparkled with a new thought. 'Nani, I've also heard that even the Pandavas from the Mahabharata returned on this day. Is it true?'

'Ah, you've heard well, my little scholar,' Nani nodded. 'It is said that the Pandavas returned from their thirteen-year exile on the day of Diwali.

The Pandavas Come Home

THIS STORY IS FROM THE EPIC MAHABHARATA. LONG ago, in the grand kingdom of Hastinapur, two sets of royal cousins were born—the five Pandavas, who were sons of King Pandu, and the hundred sons of King Dhritarashtra, who were known as Kauravas.

The Pandavas—Yudhishthira, Bhima, Arjuna, Nakula and Sahadeva—were loved by the people of Hastinapur. Many hoped to see Yudhishthira as the future king. But when their father, Pandu, died while they were still young, Dhritarashtra took over the reins of the kingdom.

The Pandavas were raised with love by their devoted mother, Kunti, who taught them values of dharma, humility and courage. While the two sets of cousins spent their childhood together and were taught by the same guru, there was an unspoken competition between them. As years passed by, the competition gave way to enmity.

The eldest Kaurava, Duryodhana, was jealous of the Pandavas, particularly Yudhishthira as his claim to the throne of Hastinapur was threatened by Yudhisthira's presence. Duryodhana plotted many devious plans against the Pandavas but was unsuccessful.

When the Pandavas transformed a piece of deserted land gifted to them by Dhritarashtra into a beautiful city of Indraprastha, Duryodhana's envy knew no bounds.

With his crafty uncle Shakuni, he created a wicked plan—a game of dice. They knew Yudhishthira's love for gambling was his only weakness, and Shakuni was a master of the game.

Duryodhana invited Yudhishthira to a game of dice at Hastinapur, and bound by royal duty, Yudhishthira accepted the invitation.

In this rigged game, Yudhishthira gambled away everything to Duryodhana—the Pandavas' kingdom, all their wealth, even their wife, Draupadi.

This game was not merely a matter of luck. It was a calculated scheme by the Kauravas to eliminate the Pandavas from taking control of the kingdom. As a consequence of the game, the Pandavas were forced into a thirteen-year exile, which included twelve years of living in the forest and the

thirteenth year in hiding. If they were discovered during their year in hiding, they would have to repeat twelve years of exile.

The Pandavas spent the last year of their exile in disguise, before returning to Hastinapur. The people of Hastinapur were delighted to have their princes back, and they decorated the whole city with diyas. It is believed that the Pandavas' homecoming happened on the night of Kartika Amavasya, the same night we now celebrate Diwali.

THE NEXT MORNING, THE CHILDREN WOKE UP TO THE smell of incense and delicious food.

In the courtyard, Nana sat on the floor, drawing colourful rangoli patterns with bowls of powdered colour and fresh flower petals.

By noon, the house was decorated, the rangoli complete and the lamps ready for the evening. Now it was time for lunch. Nani had laid the table beautifully, and it looked no less than a royal feast with kachoris, custard, dahi vadas and sweets.

Mishti began serving pooris and dahi vadas and Rahul was busy checking every plate like a little boss. Just then, Nana chuckled and said, 'Aha! You two are as wise as that clever daughter-in-law in Nani's stories!'

'What daughter-in-law, Nana?' asked Rahul.

'You don't know?' Nana said, 'Okay, let me narrate this folk story for you. But before that, do you know, Mishti, there was a time when Goddess Durga became so angry that she could have ended the world in her anger?' asked Nana.

'Do goddesses get angry too?' Mishti asked, eyes wide.

'Oh, yes, my dear! especially when someone tortures her devotees,' Nana said, in a serious tone.

The Dance of Kali in Darkness

In ancient times, the world was troubled by powerful demons. One of the most fearsome among them was Raktabija. He was a monster who had a terrifying boon—every drop of his blood that touched the ground would create a new demon just like him!

When Durga and her Matrikas attacked Raktabija, he broke out in wild laughter as thousands of Raktabija sprang up from his spilt blood.

It became impossible to defeat such a demon, as every drop of his blood gave rise to countless clones making him nearly impossible to defeat.

In her rising anger towards Raktabija, Ma Durga created a fearsome manifestation of herself known as Kali—the dark goddess.

She commanded Kali, 'O Chamunda! Open your mouth wide, and as soon as you strike Raktabija with weapons, you drink off the blood as fast as it comes out of his body.'

As the battle commenced, Kali attacked Raktabija with her deadly weapons. In her fierce form and lapping red tongue, she swiftly collected his blood in a vessel, ensuring that not a single drop fell to the ground.

After defeating Raktabija, Kali's anger soared, leading her to trample anything which came in her path. Her fury threatened to consume not just the demons, but also faultless beings.

There was only one who could calm her—Lord Shiva, her beloved.

To calm her down, Lord Shiva laid down quietly on the battlefield, right in Kali's path.

When Kali's foot touched Shiva's chest, she suddenly paused. She looked down and realised that she had stepped on the one she loved, the one who always brought peace.

In an instant, her rage melted. Kali became still, and the world was saved.

Ma Kali is one of the fierce goddesses. She is worshipped as one who destroys the evil and protects the innocent ones. Her worship during Diwali symbolises the victory of good over evil.

The Clever Daughter-in-law's Lamps

A LONG TIME AGO, THERE LIVED A PROSPEROUS KING AND his beautiful queen. One day, the queen was bathing and left her precious necklace outside. An eagle flew down, grabbed the necklace, and soared into the sky!

The king was very worried and sent his soldiers in every direction to find the missing necklace.

In the same kingdom lived a clever and kind daughter-in-law. She had a lovely rule in her home—anyone who came in from outside had to bring something useful. It could be a piece of wood, a bit of clay, or even a stone. She would then put it all to some good use.

One day, her younger brother-in-law brought home a dead snake. She told him, 'Ahh! Just throw it on the roof.'

At that exact time, the eagle flew over their house.

The necklace slipped from its claws, and fell right on the snake! The clever daughter-in-law found it and kept it safely.

When the king announced that whoever returned the queen's necklace would be rewarded, she went with her brother-in-law to the palace, to return the necklace.

The queen was delighted at her honesty and asked, 'What reward would you like?'

The daughter-in-law replied, 'On the night of Amavasya, I ask that no one else lights a lamp in the village. Only our home should have lights.'

The queen found this very strange, but agreed to the woman's wish.

That Amavasya night, Goddess Lakshmi was flying across the world, looking for a bright, clean home to enter. It was dark all around, except for that one glowing, beautiful home.

So that's where Lakshmi landed—at the daughter-in-law's home. And from that day on, the family was blessed with endless joy, wealth and happiness.

As the evening arrived, everyone changed into their colourful new clothes. The house was already buzzing with excitement, as it was the day of Lakshmi Puja, the most awaited evening of Diwali!

'Let's help Nana light the lamps!' said Rahul, carrying a tray full of clay diyas.

Twenty-two beautiful oil lamps were lit, placed for Lord Ganesha, Lord Shiva, Lord Vishnu, Goddess Lakshmi and Tulsi Ma. The rest were placed at every corner of the home.

Soon, the smell of incense and ghee filled the air, and the puja began. First, everyone prayed to Lord Ganesha, the remover of obstacles. Then came the grand puja for Goddess Lakshmi.

Mishti and Rahul looked at each other, their faces lit by the golden glow. 'This is the best Diwali ever,' proclaimed Rahul.

Day Four

Govardhan Puja—Lifting Mountains

By the time the children woke up the next morning, the sun was already high up in the sky.

'Is it still Diwali?' yawned Mishti, stretching her arms.

But as they peeked out into the courtyard, they saw something very unusual.

There was Nani, humming happily while patting down mounds of cow dung into neat, round discs.

'What is she doing?' whispered Rahul. Both of them tiptoed closer to Nani.

Before they could even ask, Nani looked up and smiled. 'Today is Govardhan Puja, the day we honour cows and the Govardhan Mountain. Come close, let me tell you all about it.'

Krishna Picks Up the Govardhan Mountain

LONG TIME AGO, THE PEOPLE OF GOKUL USED TO WORSHIP Indradev, the god of rain, paying gratitude for their good harvests.

But once, little Krishna asked, 'Why do we only thank Indra? Isn't it the cows, the fields and the Govardhan Mountain that provide us food every day? Shouldn't we be grateful to them too?'

Some nodded in agreement, touched by Krishna's wisdom, but others grew restless and scared.

One elder frowned and said, 'We should not be listening to a child for such big decisions. If Indra gets angry, he will stop the rains, and our beautiful Gokul will become a dry and deserted land.'

'How can god be angry? Is Indra like a businessman, giving rain only if we pray to him, and getting upset if we don't? A true god gives all with love, not in exchange for rituals,' said Krishna calmly.

'We are milk producers. Our lives revolve around cows, milk and butter. For us, our Ishta Devi is Gau Mata, our beloved cow who gives us milk, dung for fuel, and who loves us like a mother.'

'And who feeds her? It's the Govardhan Mountain, with its rich green grass, sweet herbs and cool waters. So shouldn't we be thanking and praying to the Govardhan Mountain instead?' asked Krishna.

The villagers, once uncertain, were now convinced by Krishna's argument.

Soon, arrangements were made to worship the Govardhan Mountain, the cows and Mother Earth.

When news reached Indra, he became furious.

'How dare they turn away from me? A mere child has misled them!' he thundered.

In his rage, he decided to teach the villagers a lesson and so with a wave of his hand, he called upon the darkest clouds at his disposal.

He summoned the Storm Gods, who galloped across skies, carrying endless rain, fierce winds and crashing thunder.

'Drown Gokul!' Indra ordered.

Within moments, the bright skies of Gokul turned black, and rains poured like rivers from the sky, flooding the land.

Houses were swept away, mud walls crumbled and belongings floated in the rising floodwaters.

Mothers held their little ones close as the fierce winds blew away the roofs, cows mooed in distress, their shelters washed away, fields that were once filled with green crops were now buried under muddy water.

'What have we done wrong?' some villagers cried.

Sitting high in the sky, Indra waited for the people to fall to their knees and beg for forgiveness.

Gokul was drowning, and people were losing their homes, thier crops and livelihood. Krishna called everyone to run towards the Govardhan Mountain.

People ran to the mountain and even brought their cattle along. Lord Krishna lifted the Govardhan Mountain on his little finger. With a gentle smile and little effort, he raised the mighty mountain high above his head, creating an umbrella-like shelter for everyone. The villagers stayed safe and dry under the hill while the storm raged on.

For seven days and nights, Krishna stood there—smiling, steady and strong, holding up the mighty Govardhan on just one finger.

Indra watched from the clouds and finally understood that this was no ordinary child. This was an avatar of the Supreme Lord.'

After the storm passed, the villagers hugged and lifted Krishna up in celebration. They thanked him for saving them and their cattle from the wrath of Indra.

NANI SMILED. 'AND THAT'S WHY TODAY, WE MAKE A little Govardhan from cow dung, decorate it, and offer our thanks to Krishna, to the cows and to Mother Earth.'

The children looked at their little hill and bowed gently.

'And what about so many cut vegetables and the chutneys you've made Nani? Do we have any more guests coming today?' asked Mishti.

'Yes, my dear, a very special guest called Krishna,' said Nani.

'So today's offerings are like saying thank you to Krishna for every day of his sacrifice?' said Mishti.

'Yes!' said Nani. 'We decorate the mountain with food, sing songs and remember Krishna's love.'

Rahul placed one more peda near the little hill and whispered, 'Here, Krishna, your missed lunch from Day 4.'

They all laughed in devotion and gratitude.

Just then, Nana came. 'Hopefully some Annakut prasad is left for me too,' he said with a smile. 'Do you know children, today is also the day of Balipratipada—the return of King Bali!'

'The return?' asked Mishti. 'Where had he gone?'

Annakut: Seven Days, Eight Feasts

For seven days and seven nights, Krishna stood there, smiling and holding the mountain on his delicate finger, without eating a single bite!

Being a very active boy, Krishna usually would eat eight times a day, but not once did he complain.

The people, cows, women and children remained safe and dry under the mountain, singing, playing and praying underneath it. They brought food for each other, but Krishna refused even a nibble as he focused solely on holding up the mountain.

The people were so full of love and gratitude for Krishna that they wanted to feed their Giridhari—the one who held the mountain.

They remembered, 7 days, 8 meals a day. That's 56 missed meals!

So they prepared Chappan Bhog, 56 delicious dishes, as an offering to say thanks to Krishna.

Sweets, savories, fruits—a mountain of food!

This mountain of food is called Annakut.

After the Annakut is prepared and offered, people perform Govardhan Aarti, and Annakut Prasad is shared with everyone.

On this day, people also bathe their cattle and put kumkum tilak and garlands on them to worship them.

The Annakut symbolises the abundance and prosperity which has been bestowed on us by nature. Many devotees do parikrama around the Govardhan Mountain and offer food to it.

The Return of Bali

THE STORY OF RAJA BALI IS ABOUT A POWERFUL, YET kind-hearted Asura king. His kingdom was full of joy. People had plenty to eat, they were happy and safe, he was deeply loved by all.

Bali was different from other Asuras. He was strong, but humble; rich but generous.

As Bali's reputation spread across different worlds, it brought a sense of fear in the hearts of the Devas. He had become more loved than they ever could!

The Devas worried that the benevolent nature of the asura might start overshadowing their own status, leading to an imbalance in the cosmos.

Bali was such a powerful ruler than even Indra started feeling threatened by him. He went to Lord Vishnu for advice. Lord Vishnu found a way out. He took on the form

of Vaaman, a humble dwarf Brahmin, and approached King Bali requesting for alms.

Bali, known for his charitable nature, offered Vaaman anything he asked for. The dwarf asked him for a piece of land that he could cover in three strides. Bali thought it was a very small request, and he happily agreed.

But as soon as the wish was granted, Vaaman's body started growing in size. Soon, it towered over the earth and reached the heavens. Bali recognised Vaaman was no other than Lord Vishnu. He felt a surge of joy that the divine had come to him.

Taking his first step, Vaaman covered the entire earth, and with his second step, he took the heavens. Finding no space left, he asked Bali where he should place his third step. King Bali humbly offered his own head.

Gratified by Bali's selflessness, Lord Vishnu gave him Patalaloka, the kingdom of the netherworlds. Lord Vishnu also blessed him with a promise that he could return to earth once a year to reunite with his beloved people. This day is celebrated as Balipratipada

Day Five

Bhai Dooj—Building Bonds

On the fifth morning, Mishti and Rahul woke up early. They quickly bathed and got ready.

Nani smiled, placing a thali in front of them.

'The fifth day of Diwali is Bhai Dooj,' she said. 'It celebrates the sacred bond between brothers and sisters.'

Rahul looked at Mishti and grinned. 'So do I get gifts too?'

Nani chuckled. 'Of course! This day is called Bhai Teeka, Bhai Phota or Bhau Beej in different parts of India. But the idea behind them all is to celebrate the love between siblings.'

Mishti took the kumkum tilak from the thali that Nani had prepared, and carefully applied a mark on Rahul's forehead. She then fed him a laddoo. 'May you always be happy, and always share your chocolates with me!' she said.

'There are some beautiful stories around this festival,' Nani continued as Rahul handed Mishti a laddoo.

'These stories are about sibling love,' said Nani. 'And I heard these stories from my grandparents. I'll tell you all of them, one by one.'

Krishna and Subhadra's Gift

After slaying the evil Narakasura, who had terrorised the heavens and abducted countless women, Lord Krishna returned on Garuda to share his triumph with his sister Subhadra.

Subhadra was beaming with pride and happiness. She had prepared a grand welcome feast for her heroic brother. Krishna arrived at her doorstep, which was adorned with beautiful rangolis made of fragrant flowers and was lit with ghee lamps, celebrating his homecoming.

She greeted him with an embrace.

In a display of affection, Subhadra had prepared a feast with all of her brother's favorite dishes. She fed them to him by her own hand. With utmost love, she applied a kumkum tilak on Krishna's forehead, invoking blessings and protection.

Seven Sisters and Their Promise

Once, there were seven sisters and their beloved younger brother. All the sisters were married and lived in different towns. When the brother was about to get married, their mother said, 'My son, your elder sisters all live far away, but your youngest sister lives nearby. Go and bring her home.'

The brother set off and arrived at his youngest sister's house. The door was shut, for she was busy performing the Bhai Dooj puja, a sacred ritual. Once the puja was done, she opened the door and was overjoyed to see her brother. She welcomed him warmly, offered him food and water, and made him comfortable.

With a smile, the brother said, 'Sister, I'm getting married! I've come to take you with me.'

The sister replied, 'Of course, I will come. But I need to take my husband's permission. You go ahead, I will take care of things here and join the celebration as soon as I can.' The sister quickly finished all her work at home and started her journey.

On the way she saw a strange man collecting porcupine thorns. She stopped and asked him, 'What are you going to do with these?'

'Keeping these thorns nearby helps protect me on the road,' said the man, holding up a small pouch. 'They may look sharp and useless, but they keep obstacles and dangers away.'

Hearing this, she thought it would be wise to keep some of them with her too. So the sister took some porcupine thorns from him, and continued her journey.

As she went ahead, she saw another man lighting a lamp and blabbering to himself, 'There are these seven sisters, who have only one beloved brother. There are four obstacles in his marriage. If someone can shield him from those obstacles, then he could be saved. Otherwise he will die.'

She asked the man, 'Who are you talking of? If there is no problem, please tell me about those obstacles.'

He said, 'In the first obstacle the gate will fall, in the second the tree will fall, and in the third the lion will carry the bridegroom from the marriage mandap. Even if he survives all three, he will die of a snakebite. Only, the thorns of the porcupine can prevent these obstacles.'

The sister hastily reached her parents' house. There, she started acting crazy, abusing people and saying mean things to them. She would appear for every ritual, to see how everything was, before letting her brother do anything.

Finally, the wedding day arrived. The groom was eager and excited. But, just before the rituals began, the sister said she wouldn't let her brother step out through the front gate, he would leave only through the back window instead.

The sister was so insistent that the brother had to go out through the window. But as he was leaving the house, suddenly the heavy front gate fell and crashed. The sister pricked the fallen door with the thorn and proceeded to lead all other rituals.

Some moments passed, and the wedding procession started. The sister insisted on going with them all.

When the procession stopped to rest under a tree, she said, 'Make my brother stand in the sun.' Everyone had to listen to the crazy woman, and they all sat down in the field.

As soon as they sat down, the tree uprooted and fell, but the guests were saved. The sister pricked the fallen tree, too, with a thorn.

After a while, the wedding rituals began. Suddenly, a lion came out of nowhere, roaring near the mandap. The sister ran after it, and threw a bundle of barley and porcupine's thorns on the lion's face. The lion got scared and ran away.

The wedding ceremony was successful. The bride and the groom returned home. After the exchange of gifts at night, the sister started saying, 'I will sleep on my brother and sister-in-law's marital bed tonight.' Everybody tried to convince her not to do so, but she would not listen to anyone.

Finally, the brother agreed to let her sleep between him and the new bride. As the night passed, both of them fell asleep, but the sister kept on singing and humming. Soon, she saw a black poisonous snake trying sneak in through the window. With one swift strike, she killed it and threw it outside in the drain. Then she walked out singing and dancing.

When her mother saw the sister, she was furious at her and said, 'Ever since you came back, you have been acting strangely, almost like you've lost your senses. Look how you are dancing at midnight, what's wrong with you?'

The sister quietly pointed to the dead snake lying nearby and then explained everything—the warning given by the strange man, and how she had done everything to protect her brother.

When her brother came to know everything, he was deeply moved. He offered her many gifts as a token of his gratitude, love and appreciation, and with a heart full of warmth and respect, he bid her farewell.

The River's Oath

ONCE, THERE WERE TWO BEST FRIENDS. ONE WAS A queen and the other was a kind woman from a humble family. One day, both found out they were going to be mothers.

They made a sweet promise to each other.

'If we both have boys, they will be best friends. If we both have girls, they will grow up like sisters. And if one has a boy and the other a girl, they will get married one day.'

Time passed. The queen gave birth to a daughter and the kind woman gave birth to a boy. When the children grew up, people began to whisper, 'Will the lovely princess really marry a boy from a humble background?'

The princess heard it and felt hurt. 'I don't want to marry someone poor!' she said.

So, a decision was made. On the holy day of Yamuna Snan, the five-day-long river bathing festival, if the boy could meet the princess before she finished her bath, they would be married. If not, they would become brother and sister.

The first day, the boy came prepared and tried his best. He pricked his finger and filled it with chili to stay awake. But the cold breeze made him sleepy, and he dozed off.

The princess came, bathed and saw him sleeping. She smiled gently, applied sandalwood to his feet, and whispered, 'I came, I bathed, I stood drying my hair. Now I return to my land.'

The second day, he lit a small fire to stay warm and awake. But again, he fell asleep.

The princess came, bathed and applied sandalwood to his knees.

'I came, I bathed, I stood drying my hair. And now I return to my land.'

The third day came. 'I must not sleep today!' the boy said to himself. He rubbed chili in his eyes to stay awake. But the cold wind calmed the burning, and his eyes closed.

The princess came once more. She bathed, and this time, put sandalwood on his chest.

'I came, I bathed, I stood drying my hair. But now I must return to my land.'

The fourth day, he sang songs all night to keep sleep away. But when morning came, he was so tired, he dozed off.

The princess bathed, and softly said, 'I came, I bathed, I stood drying my hair, and gave you coconut oil and sandal too!'

When he woke up, he was very sad.

It was the fifth day, and a final chance for the boy to meet the girl. 'I must do something different,' he thought. He sat on sharp thorns of Babool so that sleep wouldn't come. But after hours of pain, he finally fell asleep once again.

The princess came for the last time. She bathed, saw the boy sleeping and smiled kindly. She gently applied sandalwood to his forehead and said, 'I came, I bathed, I stood drying my hair and I put sandalwood on your forehead, like a sister.'

Then she softly woke him and said, 'You are now my brother.'

The boy was sad. But when the queen and her old friend heard everything, their hearts were full.

They smiled and said, 'Let them be loving siblings forever!'

So, on the next festival day, the princess invited him home like a true brother. She cooked food with her own hands, fed him with love, and placed a tilak on his forehead.

Everyone clapped and cheered. And from that day on, they were family in every way that mattered.

And they all lived happily ever after.

Yama and Yami's Eternal Bond

IN MANY PARTS OF INDIA, BHAI DOOJ IS CALLED YAMDWITIYA. It celebrates the bond between Yama, the god of death, and his twin sister, Yami, who is also known as Yamuna.

Yama and Yami were children of Surya Dev, the sun god. They were very close. But after Yama became the lord of death, he hardly found time to visit his sister.'

It is said that Yama was so preoccupied that, despite numerous invitations, he couldn't visit Yami.

One day, Yami lovingly invited her brother to her home yet again.

However, this time, he decided to surprise her with a visit. As he started on his journey to Yami's home, he did something that astonished even the gods.

Yamraj was so happy to be meeting his sister that he opened the doors of hell, liberating the souls trapped within. It was a gesture of mercy, for even the lord of death has a compassionate heart.

His arrival brought an instant smile of joy to Yami's face. She greeted him with a tilak on his forehead and showered him with Akshat, symbolising her love and respect.

Yamraj was so pleased that before leaving, he gave her money and said, 'Sister, ask for something.'

Yamuna said, 'O, my great brother, give this blessing to all the brothers and sisters who take bath on Bhai Dooj at Vishrant Ghat of Yamuna River in Mathura. They will not have to go to Yamlok.'

Yamraj said, 'Sister, I have accepted your wish. Also, on this day, the brother who goes to his sister's place, eats food and gets tilak done, would be blessed with a long life.'

Legends Beyond Diwali

‘There are so many legends around Diwali,’ added Papa, joining them with a tray of sweets.

‘Different communities across India, and even around the world, celebrate this festival of lights for so many different reasons.

‘Do you know how the Jains celebrate Diwali?’ asked Papa.

‘Jains? Like my friend Parth?’ said Rahul.

‘Exactly,’ said Papa. ‘For them, Diwali is the night when Vardhaman Mahavira, their great teacher, found eternal peace.’

‘Papa, who is Vardhaman?’ Rahul looked up with wide eyes and asked.

‘Ah, Vardhaman, he was a special child,’ Papa began.

Lord Mahavira's Nirvana

A LONG, LONG TIME AGO, IN THE KINGDOM OF Kundagrama, there lived a kind and noble couple, King Siddhartha and Queen Trishala. One night, Queen Trishala had fourteen mythical dreams. In the dream she saw lions, elephants, flowers and even a rain of jewels!

The next day, the minister of the kingdom said, 'This is a sign of the arrival of a great soul! He will bring light to the world.'

And soon after, a beautiful baby boy was born to the couple. They named him Vardhaman, which means ever-growing. From the moment he was born, joy, peace and goodness began growing everywhere in the kingdom. Little Vardhaman wasn't like other children. He was kind to animals and birds. He never even hurt an ant. If he saw someone sad, he would stop and help.

One day, while he was playing with his friends, a snake slithered close by. The children screamed and ran away, but not Vardhaman. He calmly looked at the snake and said, 'Go in peace, little one.'

And the snake calmy slithered away.

When Vardhaman grew up to be a young man, a celestial being came down to test his courage. He disguised himself as a scary monster with wild hair and big teeth.

Everyone ran. But Vardhaman stood firm.

He said gently, 'I am not afraid. Truth is stronger than fear.'

The monster smiled, took his real form, and bowed to the brave little boy.

As Vardhaman grew older, he didn't become proud or bossy like some princes do. He became even more gentle and more thoughtful.'

At the age of thirty, something very sad happened to Vardhaman. Both his parents, King Siddhartha and Queen Trishala, passed away. So often Vardhaman would sit in solitude and think about life.

He would sit under a tree, watching birds fly, ants work, clouds drift and wonder.

'Why do people fight? Why do animals get hurt? Is there a way to live with kindness, always?'

His heart ached to find the answers, and one day he renounced everything he had. He gave away all his robes,

jewels and royal comforts. He wore only a simple cloth, had no shoes, no umbrella and carried no food.

He walked barefoot through forests and villages, slept under trees and never hurt a single creature.

For many years, he didn't speak much. He let the nature and silence teach him.

Sometimes people were unkind to him. They teased him, shouted at him, or even threw stones at him.

But Vardhaman stayed calm. He forgave them. He believed that true courage is staying peaceful, even when others are not.

One quiet night, after years of walking, fasting and thinking deeply, Vardhaman sat beneath a tree, and something incredible happened.

He found the truth of life. A deep, peaceful joy lit up inside him. He became Mahavira. He found Moksha—freedom from all sorrow.

Jains believe that Lord Mahavira attained moksha on the day of Diwali at Pawapuri in Bihar, after years of spiritual practice.

Jain community celebrates Diwali in spiritual reflection, by fasting and reciting the holy scriptures. They also visit Jain temples, light lamps and distribute sweets in remembrance of this significant event in their spiritual history.

Just then, Mishti sat up excitedly.

'Nani, do you know, even Sikh people celebrate Diwali! Our friend Agam told us a story. It's really cool!'

Nani smiled, 'Of course! The story of Bandi Chhor Diwas, right?'

'Yes!' said Mishti.

Rahul scratched his head, looking puzzled. 'I don't know this story,' he said. 'What's Bandi Chhor Diwas?'

Mishti gently patted his back. 'I can narrate the story to you, only if you don't interrupt me.'

'I promise not to,' said Rahul.

Bandi Chhor Divas: The Day of Release

IT WAS DURING THE TIME OF THE MUGHAL RULE. EMPEROR Jahangir would often imprison individuals from various sects, to pressurise them into converting to Islam.

One day, Jahangir got to know about the brave Sikh Guru, Guru Hargobind Sahib Ji, and how his people adored him. He was jealous and afraid of the Guru's growing popularity, and he summoned Guru Hargobind Sahib Ji and put him under house arrested in his huge fort.

Guru Hargobind found out that he was not alone there. Fifty-two other kings were imprisoned in the same fort.

However, Emperor Jahangir had some sympathy for Guru Hargobind, as he knew him to be a noble soul. He offered to release him, but Guru Hargobind insisted that

he will leave his cell only if his fellow prisoners were also set free.

Jahangir agreed to this condition, but added that as many who could hold onto the Guru's cloak would be allowed to leave with him.

In a clever act of compassion, Guru Hargobind had a special cloak made with fifty-two strings, allowing each of the fifty-two kings to hold onto a string, and walk out of the prison alongside him.

This remarkable event is why the day is celebrated as Bandi Chhor Diwas, or the day of liberation. Sikhs around the world honour it by lighting lamps in their homes.

'Do you know, my dears, there's also a calendar that started because of King Vikramaditya?' Nani asked.

Rahul's eyes widened.

'Wait, Vikramaditya made a calendar?' Mishti looked puzzled.

Nani chuckled. 'Yes, it's called the Vikram Samvat.'

'By the way, do you know, Nepal also celebrates Diwali in its own way?' said Nani. 'Diwali in Nepal is also called Tihar and it is celebrated with great joy and reverence.'

Vikramaditya and the New Calendar

LONG, LONG AGO, IN THE CITY OF UJJAIN, LIVED KING Gandharvasena. One day, he made a big mistake. He kidnapped a monk's sister. The monk, Kalakacharya, needed help to save her. So, he called upon the Shakas, warriors from a foreign land.

The Shakas attacked Ujjain with great force.

King Gandharvasena fled to save his life, and the Shakas took over the city. As the years passed, Gandharvasena's son, Vikramaditya, grew up to be a brave and strong man. He wanted to win back his father's kingdom.

He fought the Shakas and won. On the day of his coronation, he started a new calendar. We know it as Vikram Samvat.

Also known as the Vikrami calendar, it is the historical Hindu calendar in the Indian subcontinent. It's a lunisolar calendar and has no dates like one to thirty or thirty-one, but only lunar days like Dwitiya, Tritiya, Purnima or Amavasya.

Loyal subjects of King Vikramaditya were so overjoyed by his coronation that they illuminated the kingdom with countless lamps, creating a dazzling display.

Vikram Samvat, the ancient lunisolar calendar, is used in many parts of India and Nepal. What makes it special is that it follows both the moon's phases and the sun's journey across the sky, balancing the lunar months with solar seasons. This calendar is approximately 57 years ahead of the Gregorian calendar. Festivals, harvests and religious rituals in Hindu tradition often follow this calendar, keeping nature and culture beautifully in sync. It's also part of the Panchanga, the traditional Hindu calendar used in astrology, and helps decide important timings, or muhurtas, for rituals, weddings and more!

The Nepali Festival of Tihar

THE FIRST DAY OF TIHAR IS KNOWN AS KAAG TIHAR, which translates to crow Tihar. On this day, devotees honour crows and ravens. In Hindu belief system, these birds are regarded as the messengers of Yama. Offerings of grains, seeds and sweets are laid out on rooftops and streets to attract them.

On the second day of Tihar, known as Kukur Tihar, which means dog Tihar, dogs are honoured for their loyalty and friendship. People worship their dogs by adorning them with marigold garlands, applying teeka on their foreheads and feeding them special treats.

The third day is called Gai Tihar or cow Tihar. Cows, which are sacred animals in Hinduism, are worshipped on this day. They're decorated with garlands, teeka is applied on them, and they're offered treats.

These three days of festivities come to an end with the main Diwali celebration on the third day, when Lakshmi is worshipped and homes are illuminated with lights.

'MISHTI AND RAHUL, NOT ALL PEOPLE CELEBRATE the festival of Diwali,' said Nani softly.

'One of my friends, who spent her childhood in the mountains, told me about this tribe in the forests of Kumaon, called the Tharu tribe, who do not light lamps on Diwali.'

'Wow! I haven't heard that before. But why so, Nani? Are they angry at someone?' asked Rahul

'Do you remember the Ramayana story about how Lord Rama went looking for Sita?' The children nodded, and Nani began telling them the story ...

The Unhappy Diwali

Ma Sita was held captive by Ravana. Rama and Lakshmana, in their search for Sita, had found out that she was imprisoned in Lanka.

Lord Rama needed to cross the ocean to reach Lanka. He seeked the help of the water god, Varuna, to give way to them through the ocean but he would not listen to them.

Rama grew stern. 'If Varuna won't listen,' he said, 'then I shall dry up the sea!' Then he readied his powerful Brahmastra, an unstoppable weapon.

Just then Varuna appeared with folded hands.

'O Rama,' said Varuna, 'forgive me. I was not being proud, I was merely following the natural course of dharma. The laws of nature are made by you, and I must obey them.'

Rama understood. But the Brahmastra, once loaded, couldn't be put away. It had to be fired somewhere.

Rama directed the arrow towards a dry land far away. When the Brahmastra hit the ground, it scorched the earth, dried up rivers and created a vast desert—the Thar Desert.

It is believed that the ancestors of the Tharu tribe lived in that region and many perished in that fiery storm.

But a few survived, who later settled in the Himalayan foothills. There they found rivers, trees and quiet valleys where they could begin life again.

Since then, the Tharu tribe has mourned this day. For them, Diwali isn't a festival of lights; it's a day to remember their ancestors.

And that's why, for generations, many Tharu families have not celebrated Diwali with lights. Instead, on this day, they offer sweets and roti to their ancestors.

By now the evening had set in and everyone gathered at the verandah for tea, warm samosas and gulab jamuns. Even the pet dog Temper joined them.

'Temper reminds me of a short legend narrated by my father,' said Nana laughingly.

When Farm Animals Complained

THIS HAPPENED WHEN THE WORLD WAS STILL VERY NEW, and god had just created humans. In the beginning, god gave humans food to eat. But after a while, he told them, 'Now you must grow your own food.'

So the humans tried, but it was really hard work.

They didn't have the right tools, and they struggled a lot. Tired and worried, they prayed to Lord Shiva for help.

Kind and wise, Lord Shiva listened to their prayers. He sent them animals such as cows, bulls, goats and sheep, to help them with farming. But he also gave a warning to the humans.

'Treat these animals with love and kindness,' he said.

At first, everything went well. The animals helped in the fields; people grew lots of food and everyone was happy.

But then, things started to change. People became lazy and greedy. They made the animals work more and more, gave them little food and didn't keep their sheds clean. The poor animals were fed up with such disregard.

So the animals decided to do something very brave. They prayed to Lord Shiva and called out to him.

'Dear lord,' they said, 'we are being overworked and not cared for. Please help us!'

Lord Shiva listened carefully and said, 'I will visit the earth on the no-moon night of Kartik. I will see everything with my own eyes.'

That's the very night on which we celebrate Diwali!

When people heard that Lord Shiva was coming, they got scared. They rushed to clean the sheds, fed the animals the best food and even decorated their horns with bright red vermilion. Lamps were lit all around the sheds, and everything looked beautiful.

When Lord Shiva arrived, he saw the animals were finally happy and well cared for. People were praying to him as Pashupati—the lord of animals.

From that day on, this special event became a yearly tradition. It is now celebrated as the Sohrai festival, mainly in the eastern states of India, like Jharkhand, West Bengal, Odisha and Chhattisgarh.

On this day, people thank and decorate their cattle, feed them lovingly, and clean their homes and sheds.

'Nani, Diwali is over,' Rahul sighed. 'We'll have to go back to school, to uniforms and to homework. No more lights, no more laddoos,' he mumbled.

Nani chuckled softly, wrapping her arm around Rahul's shoulders. 'Arre, Rahul, who said Diwali is over everywhere?'

Rahul looked up, eyes wide. 'What do you mean?'

'Well, in some places, Diwali is celebrated a month later than the real Diwali!'

Rahul sat up straight. 'How?'

'In parts of Himachal Pradesh and Uttarakhand,' Nani said, 'people celebrate something called Budhi Diwali exactly one month after the regular Diwali.'

Budhi Diwali

When Lord Rama, Lakshmana and Sita returned to Ayodhya after defeating Ravana, the people welcomed them with joy.

But the news of Lord Rama's return travelled slowly, especially to the mountains. It was exactly one month later that they received the news of their favourite prince's homecoming.

'So the people there lit their own lamps and celebrated Diwali, with the same joy and love, but a little later. That's why it's called Budhi Diwali—the old or delayed Diwali.'

Some other legends say the mountain people were busy harvesting, and didn't get time for Diwali.

In places like Shimla, Kullu, Jaunsar-Bawar and Manshaari, it's celebrated with bonfires, nagadas, folk dances and plays. People throw pinewood and dry grass into the fire, instead of bursting crackers.

'Wow!' said Rahul. 'So even when our Diwali ends, theirs will start soon'

Nani nodded. 'Yes, and it teaches us that just like Diwali, light keeps finding a way.'

Nani pulled all the children into her warm arms and said softly, 'I am seventy-five Diwalis old now, children! And this festival of lights, year after year, has taught me one simple truth—to live each moment with love, gratitude and honesty in our hearts.'

Outside, the night sky twinkled. The last of the leftover crackers sparkled and popped in the distance.

And far away, in the quiet hills, a second Diwali was just around the corner!

Author's Note

Dear readers,

As we come to end of the book, you must have understood that there are a lot of entertaining and fascinating facts about Diwali that we can all learn a lot from. Yet, I am also sure that there might be many more legends and stories behind this beautiful festival of light.

But at its core, Diwali serves as a reminder that a single act of love can light up any heart full of sorrow, and that a single spark of light can erase the darkness of a million years.

Therefore, when you light the lamps this Diwali, my dear children, keep in mind the inspirational stories and thought-provoking lessons they impart.

Allow Diwali's light to fill your life with happiness, optimism and virtue.

A very happy Diwali, to all!

Acknowledgements

WITH FOLDED HANDS, I BOW IN GRATITUDE TO THE great rishis and yogis of the past, whose wisdom, devotion and vision preserved the stories and legends that continue to illuminate our lives. Their words are the eternal lamps that have kept the spirit of Diwali alive across ages.

I am thankful to all those who carried Diwali and other festivals in their hearts and shared their essence across the world, keeping the flame of tradition burning bright in every corner.

To my family—my husband, Samir, and my two boys—thank you for your patience, love and constant encouragement. Your thoughtful suggestions and the quiet moments you sacrificed while I worked on this draft, have made this book possible.

A heartfelt thanks to my publisher Westland and especially Vidhi Bhargava, my editor and publisher, for her tireless hand-holding throughout this journey. Your faith and persistence have been invaluable in shaping this book into its present form.